This dragon book belongs to:

....

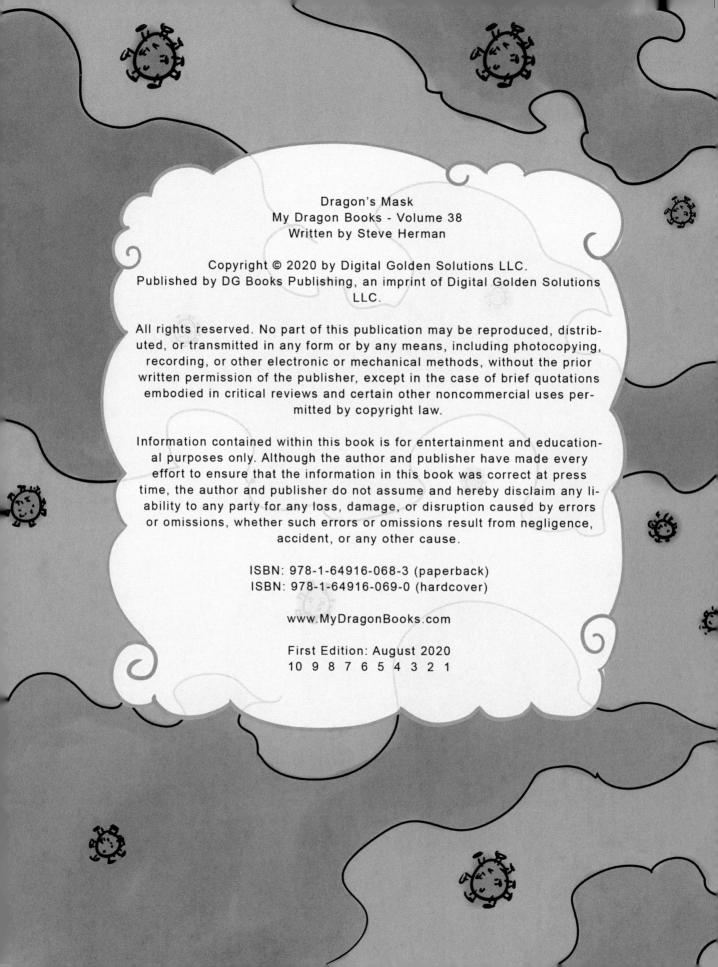

Dragon's Mask
My Dragon Books - Volume 38
Written by Steve Herman

ISBN: 978-1-64916-068-3 (paperback)
ISBN: 978-1-64916-069-0 (hardcover)

www.MyDragonBooks.com

First Edition: August 2020
10 9 8 7 6 5 4 3 2 1

It took a while to train him,
for a dragon must be taught
About the way he should behave
and ways that he should not.

And staying in the house just as often as he could – Although he didn't like it, Diggory understood.

But after weeks of staying in,
the days grew dull and long,
And dragons need to play outdoors
so they grow big and strong.

Mother bought us both a mask –
One was dragon size –
Then she sent us out to play
and get some exercise.

Diggory Doo said, "Let's play tag!"
(That's his favorite game),
Then, guess what – my dragon *sneezed!* –
Out shot a burst of flame!

Diggory got a brand new mask;
I told him, "Pay attention!
Be careful how you treat your mask!
Practice fire prevention!"

Then Diggory moved his mask
so that it covered up his eye –
"AAAARGH!" he said, "Let's play pirates!"
but I answered with a sigh –

Another time I noticed that when he began to cough, Diggory Doo reached for his mask and tried to take it off.

Diggory pulled my mask
just as far as it would go,
Stretching the elastic –
Then he laughed and let it go.

It was brightly colored
and had stripes of blue and green;
My dragon said,
"I think that mask's the best I've ever seen!"

Diggory told his friend,
"I like how your mask is made,"
Then Diggory Doo took off his mask
and asked his friend to trade.

"No!", I yelled, "You can't trade masks! Diggory Doo, Gee Whiz! Your friend could get your germs, and also you could get his."

I asked him, "What if you were sick, but didn't know it yet? Without a mask, you'd spread your germs to everyone you met."

"Or if someone else were sick,
they'd spread their germs to you.
But if you both wear a mask,
it keeps the germs from getting through."

"Don't stand too close to others;
wash your hands a lot –
These are helpful ways
to keep the germs from getting caught."

"Staying home, washing hands,
wearing masks when we go out
Are ways to stop the virus –
They work, I have no doubt."

Diggory asked, "Drew, do you know
if it will be the rule
That we still have to wear a mask
when we go back to school?"

I answered, "Diggory Doo,
I think it's possible that we will,
Until the virus is gone,
we don't know who might be ill."

Then Diggory said, "Hey, Drew, don't some heroes wear a mask?!" "Yes, some heroes do," I said, "but tell me why you ask."

He said "I am a **hero**!
With my mask, I'll start today!
It will be my **super** power
to drive the germs away!"

Made in the USA
Middletown, DE
03 September 2021